Paddy's First Day
At Hilltop School

by Sean Rooney

Strategic Book Publishing

Strategic Book Publishing
An imprint of Strategic Book Group
P.O. Box 333
Durham CT 06422
www.StrategicBookGroup.com

ISBN: 978-1-60860-115-8   1-60860-115-3

Printed in the United States of America

Illustrations art, book cover art and book layout by
kalpart team - www.kalpart.com

To my friend Alexandra, for helping me
accomplish this dream.
Your encouragement kept me going.

Acknowledgements

Thanks to my brother and all of his friends for making these characters come alive.

Once upon a time, there was a muskrat named Paddy who lived in Tennessee. He had cerebral palsy and couldn't walk like other kids, so he drove a bright yellow wheelchair with green racing stripes. Paddy was in second grade and had lots of friends at school.

One day, he found out that he was moving to South Carolina because his dad changed jobs. He did not take the news well. He remembered what a tough time he had when he started kindergarten. It always took him a while to get to know the other kids because they were afraid of his wheelchair. He did not want to go through that again.

"Don't worry," his parents said. "You'll be fine, Paddy."

So before leaving, he gave his friends his new address, and said goodbye to all of them. "I'll keep in touch," he assured them.

Paddy's mom said, "It's time we head out."

As the family car pulled away, Paddy waved goodbye to his friends and neighbors.

They finally arrived at their new house. It was bigger than his old house. Paddy even had his own room. After getting everything unpacked, Paddy wanted some alone time before dinner. He drove his wheelchair into his room to play a videogame. He was already missing his friends in Tennessee.

That night, when his mom was getting him ready for bed, he told her he was nervous about starting a new school.

"Don't worry," his mom said as she helped him out of his wheelchair. "Your aide, Miss Lyle, will get you off the bus tomorrow, and she will take you to your class. She'll be there to help you when you need something."

The next morning, Paddy was the first one awake. For good luck, his mom dressed him in his favorite tie-dyed tee shirt. She also made him his favorite breakfast of chocolate chip pancakes to make him feel better. Soon after his last bite; the bus pulled up to get him.

His parents walked out with him, gave him his books and lunch money, and strapped his wheelchair down so that he could have a safe ride. They waved goodbye to him as the bus drove off.

At the next stop, Paddy watched as other kids got onto the bus. One boy pushed his way to the back and sat down next to Paddy. His name was Luke, the skunk. Luke laughed at Paddy, and made fun of how he looked. He took Paddy's lunch money away from him and leaned back into his seat. Paddy tried to get it back, but he couldn't reach him.

Soon the bus pulled up to the school. Paddy thought it looked bigger than his old school. His aide, Miss Lyle, the beaver, was there to receive him, just like his mom said. She introduced herself with a big smile and said, "Welcome to Hilltop School."

Paddy told the bus driver and Miss Lyle what happened on the bus with Luke. The bus driver said that she'd try to get it solved. Miss Lyle took him inside to his classroom, and guess who was in the class across the hall? Luke!

Paddy drove to his desk. Next to him was a tall, skinny rabbit.

"Hi. my name is Austin. What's yours?" he said.

"My name's Paddy."

"I like your tie-dyed tee shirt," said Austin.

"Thanks," said Paddy. "Your shirt's cool too."

Paddy's teacher, Mrs. Huggins the fox, introduced him to the rest of the class.

The morning went by quickly. Mrs. Huggins was very nice, and stopped by Paddy's desk often to see how he was doing.

Finally, it was lunchtime. Paddy's new friend, Austin, sat with him. They saw Luke sitting at another table. Paddy told Austin what happened on the bus that morning, and Austin went over to tell Luke to give Paddy his lunch money back.

"You need to stop bullying others. I'm tired of you treating other people badly, especially handicapped people," Austin said.

Luke gave back Paddy his lunch money, and went to his seat.

Miss Lyle said, "It looks like you got your lunch money back with a little help from your new friend Austin." Paddy looked over at Austin and knew that he'd made a friend for life.

LaVergne, TN USA
14 February 2010
173056LV00001B